WHY DO ANIMALS HIDE?

Robin Koontz

Rourke
Educational Media

rourkeeducationalmedia.com

Scan for Related Titles
and Teacher Resources

Teaching Focus:
Concepts of Print- Have students find capital letters and punctuation in a sentence. Ask students to explain the purpose for using them in a sentence.

Before Reading:

Building Academic Vocabulary and Background Knowledge
Before reading a book, it is important to set the stage for your child or student by using pre-reading strategies. This will help them develop their vocabulary, increase their reading comprehension, and make connections across the curriculum.
1. Read the title and look at the cover. *Let's make predictions about what this book will be about.*
2. Take a picture walk by talking about the pictures/photographs in the book. Implant the vocabulary as you take the picture walk. Be sure to talk about the text features such as headings, Table of Contents, glossary, bolded words, captions, charts/diagrams, and Index.
3. Have students read the first page of text with you then have students read the remaining text.
4. Strategy Talk – use to assist students while reading.
   - Get your mouth ready
   - Look at the picture
   - Think…does it make sense
   - Think…does it look right
   - Think…does it sound right
   - Chunk it – by looking for a part you know
5. Read it again.
6. After reading the book complete the activities below.

Content Area Vocabulary
Use glossary words in a sentence.

camouflage
disguises
mimic
predators
prey
terrain

After Reading:

Comprehension and Extension Activity
After reading the book, work on the following questions with your child or students in order to check their level of reading comprehension and content mastery.
1. *What animal in the book disguises itself to look like seaweed?* (Inferring)
2. *What disguises do spider crabs use to stay safe from predators?* (Asking questions)
3. *Name two animals in the book that use flowers to disguise themselves.* (Text to self connection)
4. *Why do animals need to disguise themselves?* (Summarize)

Extension Activity
Animals need to camouflage or disguise themselves to stay safe. There are many different ways they do this. Take a walk in your yard or another place, such as a park, where there may be insects or other animals. Bring a notebook, a pencil, and a magnifying glass and see if you can find anything hiding or disguising itself on plants, leaves, flowers, or shrubs. Record your findings in your notebook.

Table of Contents

Clever Critters

Matching twigs! A clever trick.

Is it a bug? Or is it a stick?

Can you see the insect hiding in the photo? Walking sticks and many other insects hide. They use different kinds of **camouflage**.

A lot of animals use camouflage to hide from **predators.** Many animals also use camouflage to hide from their **prey.**

A fawn, or baby deer, has white spots on its brown fur. The spots make it difficult for predators to see the fawn.

Leopards, tigers, cheetahs, and other wildcats have spots or stripes. The patterns help them hide in their surroundings.

Alligators and crocodiles have gray and brown scaly skin. They can look like logs floating in the water. A crocodile may put sticks on its head to attract nesting birds.

Many other animals have colors, shapes, and patterns that blend with their surroundings. A walking leaf insect even sways like a leaf blowing in the wind.

Owls have feathers that match where they rest or watch for prey. Owls can also puff up or make themselves thinner to help them blend in.

The pygmy seahorse hides so well that it was only discovered recently on sea fans collected for study.

The tiny pygmy seahorse attaches to sea fans. Its color and shape look like a branch of the plant.

A reef stonefish looks like a real stone with its bumpy skin. It can fool its prey and also hide from predators.

Flounders hide in the sandy seabed.
They can make their skin lighter or darker
to match the sand.

Chromatophores are special skin cells that change color when they receive messages from the animal's brain.

A leafy sea dragon's body trails a mass of colorful tassels that look like seaweed.

Hide and Seek

A flower mantis looks like a beautiful flower. It hides on a real flower and tricks prey insects into getting too close.

A goldenrod crab spider also blends with flowers. When an insect comes along, the sneaky spider snags it.

Climate change affects the snowshoe hare and other Arctic prey animals. They are in danger when snowfall comes late or melts early.

A snowshoe hare changes from snowy white in winter to forest brown in summer. So does the Arctic fox, one of the hare's predators.

Daring Disguises

Spider crabs attach things to their shells. Predators can't spot them in their **disguises**.

A lot of animals **mimic** other animals that taste bad or are dangerous.

A snake caterpillar can look and behave like a slithering snake about to bite!

Cuttlefish are master mimics. They can instantly change their color and shape to blend with their **terrain**.

Cuttlefish often confuse an enemy by changing so quickly. Poof!

The animal world is filled with hiding tricks. It's a clever way for them to survive.

Squids and octopuses are related to cuttlefish. Many of them also have amazing color and shape-shifting abilities.

Photo Glossary

camouflage (KAM-uh-flahzh): Camouflage is a disguise or natural coloring that allows animals or people to hide.

disguises (diss-GIZE-iz): Disguises change the appearance of something.

mimic (MIM-ik): Imitating another person or animal.

predators (PRED-uh-turz): Predators hunt other animals for food.

prey (PRAY): An animal hunted by other animals for food.

terrain (tuh-RAYN): Terrain is an area of land.

Index

Websites to Visit

gws.ala.org/category/animals
kids.nationalgeographic.com
a-z-animals.com

Meet The Author!
www.meetREMauthors.com

About the Author

Robin Koontz is a freelance author/illustrator/designer of a wide variety of nonfiction and fiction books, educational blogs, and articles for children and young adults. Her title, *Leaps and Creeps - How Animals Move to Survive*, was an Animal Behavior Society Outstanding Children's Book Award Finalist.

Edited by: Keli Sipperley
Cover design, interior design and art direction: Nicola Stratford
www.nicolastratford.com

Library of Congress PCN Data

Why Do Animals Hide?/ Robin Koontz
(Why Do Animals...)
ISBN 978-1-68191-729-0 (hard cover)
ISBN 978-1-68191-830-3 (soft cover)
ISBN 978-1-68191-924-9 (e-Book)
Library of Congress Control Number: 2016932653

Rourke Educational Media
Printed in the United States of America, North Mankato, Minnesota

© 2017 Rourke Educational Media

www.rourkeeducationalmedia.com

PHOTO CREDITS: Cover © David Dohnal; Page 4 © Brian Lasenby, Page 5 © Critterbiz; Page 6 © Jessica Ney (cheetah), Zack Frank (spider), Page 7 © Sean Lema; Page 8 © Aedka Studio, Page 9 © David Dohnal; Page 10 © Dan Exton, Page 11 © Kristina Vackova; Page 12 © Vilainecrevette, Page 13 © Kris Wiktor; Page 14 © Sebastian Janicki, Page 15 © Henrik Larsson; Page 16 © Ian Maton, Page 17 © kevin wise; Page 19 © Mathisa; Page 20/21 © cbpix (cuttlefish), Konrad Mostert (octopus). All photos from Shutterstock.com

Also Available as:
ROURKE'S
e-Books